a pretty thing in the middle of nowhere

a collection of sapphic poems

by Tamara Ali

a pretty thing in the middle of nowhere.

Written by Tamara Ali.

Paperback ISBN: 978-976-97420-0-0

Edited and proofread by Shurland James Jr (The Grammar Trini).

Cover design by Yearwood Graphic Design.

Acknowledgements

No matter how many poems I wrote for this book, my favourite pieces of art during the writing process would forever be the friendships that kept me happy in the middle of the heartaches. Alexia, Aruna, Beyonce, Jeevana, Jerissa, Kandis, Sahrya, and Shelli. I love you all! I also want to thank my family for continuing to support me in my writing adventures. Shout out to my writer-friends, Aminah and Keeron and their poetry books that gave me inspiration to write my own. Thank you to every single homophobic person; you inspire me to be gayer every day. Thank you to my editor/proofreader, and to my cover designer. Most of all, thank you to my readers!

Table of Contents

Part One

Part Two

Part Three

For every girl who's ever loved a girl, but
never loved herself as easily.

a pretty thing in the middle of nowhere

Part One

*To meet you, was to love you instantly and
forever.*

a pretty thing in the middle of nowhere

For Her

As I write these poems, I need you to know,

most of them – not all - I wrote for her.

Most of them – not all – I wrote in tears.

Some of them – not all – I wrote while
angry.

Most of them – not all – I wrote because I
had something to say to her.

I had the words, but I did not have the
courage.

As I tell you a story, I need you to know,

I loved her, even when she was the
antagonist.

I titled this poem

For ▬▬▬▬▬

a pretty thing in the middle of nowhere

But then I saw her name written across the page and my stomach formed knots, and I had to delete it.

I title this poem

For Her

She knows how to spell her name.

when the sun met the moon

When the Sun met the Moon,

the mortals called it an eclipse.

But the Sun – she called it love.

It wasn't love at first sight. It was better.

To meet you, was to love you instantly and
forever.

It was the day before Valentine's.

The day before love bloomed.

The day I first spoke to the girl who was too
precious to be mine.

The day my heart would be forever doomed.

I should've taken that as a sign.

I shouldn't have gotten so nervous when
she took the seat next to mine.

She asked if she could write in my
notebook.

I told her, "You could do whatever you
want."

And she giggled.

She took my words and took them seriously.

Eventually, she did whatever she wanted
with my heart,

and I let her because I always keep my
word.

That February 13th, I told her,

"You could do whatever you want."

I always keep my word,

yet she took my words and ran.

When I built up the courage to talk to her,

all I could vomit out were jokes.

She laughed, but she laughs at everything.

a pretty thing in the middle of nowhere

She told me that she likes girls.

I didn't tell her that I liked her,

because in the same breath,

she told me that she had a boy-friend.

That February 13th, I fell in love.

But it wasn't at first sighting.

It was something better.

It was like our souls had finally reunited.

That February 13th was not the first day I met her.

But it was the first day I knew her.

a pretty thing in the middle of nowhere

The song I'll never listen to

It's a frustration, really, to see a girl so beautiful and know that I cannot give her my everything because her heart is already in the hands of another. It's a shame, really, to waste skin that soft on a man's rough touch. It's pathetic, really, to pen her a love letter she'll never read. I'm frustrated, but she's still beautiful. It's shameful, but she's still his. This is pathetic, but I'm still poetic. She reminds me of a pretty little bird. She likes that song. I've never listened to it, and I never will. I don't know much about her yet, but I know that she likes that song. So, I don't ever want to listen to it because I don't ever want to know her wrong.

hers is a yellow flower

my body is a whorehouse, unable to make
you stay but can always make you come

my mind is a racetrack, unable to think as
quickly as it reacts

my heart is a tombstone, unable to leave
from the ground that holds its buried
memories

my heart is a tombstone, heavy in my chest

my heart is a place of eternal grief

a place decorated with flowers and kind
words to distract from its sadness

a place that is not the peaceful home of a
body, but the lonely cage of a soul

a pretty thing in the middle of nowhere

her body is comfort food, craving my
gluttony

her mind is a chess game, strategic with
every move – a game I always lose

my heart is a tombstone

hers is a yellow flower

a delicate happiness sprinkled over my cold
corpse

a yellow flower left to wither away when it
realises that my heart is not a garden

it is not a home

it is only a grave.

God Made Girls

Boys were made to rule the world.

To keep the boys' company, God made girls.

Boys were made to make the money.

To spend it, God made girls.

Boys were made to carry on their father's

last name.

To carry the child, God made girls.

But who made the boys who would rather

sweep the house than go to war?

Who made the girls who would rather die

childless than live as "his wife"?

Did they make themselves that way after

seeing it on TV?

But why would anyone choose to be gay

when the gays are always bullied?

Me personally, I'm going to marry a man.

a pretty thing in the middle of nowhere

However, I've been diagnosed with
'bisexuality',

I think that means that I can turn into a
lesbian simply by touching a pretty girl's
hand.

Do lesbians even hold hands?

I've always been taught how to be a girl.

And of course, my girlhood was validated
once I earned the attention of a boy.

I've always been taught that I was made for
a boy, like how Eve was made for Adam.

I've only been shown the movies on how to
win the *boy*; no one taught me how to be a
lesbian.

I am not a lesbian! I'm just dramatic! Maybe
when God made me, he misspelt *thespian*!

A lesbian would know how to be the boy and
take the lead and kiss her; I barely know
how to hold her hand.

a pretty thing in the middle of nowhere

Still, I must ask,

if I wasn't made for girls,

why does it feel like

she was made for me?

Man in a Dress

Trapped inside a pink box,

on display like a doll.

My attempt at femininity is

constantly mocked.

Still, do not call me a tomboy,

I hate to kick a ball.

What am I? Why must I choose?

There must be another colour

between the pink and the blue.

There must be something beyond

the binary.

This dress is pretty, but it does not

flatter me.

This shirt is comfortable, but I don't

want people to stare.

There must be something else I can

wear.

She's as pretty as a kiss

She's as pretty as a first kiss.

The kind of first kiss that you have at a
sleepover at thirteen.

The kind of first kiss that is as special as it is
awkward.

The kind of first kiss that you defend to
every kiss that comes afterwards:

"that doesn't count as a real kiss"

but it does.

She's the kind of kiss that counts.

She's as pretty as a flower.

The kind of flower you pick for its beauty
and keep for its meaning.

The kind of flower you grieve for when it
dies.

a pretty thing in the middle of nowhere

She's as pretty as a winter wonderland.

The kind of winter I've never seen.

The kind of snow that has never touched my hands.

She's as pretty as the winter you only see on TV.

She's as pretty as the mean girls in my favourite movie.

She's as pretty as the moon.

There's only one moon.

She's prettier than it.

She's as pretty as a love story.

The kind of love story that you wish to be real.

The kind of love story that ends.

a pretty thing in the middle of nowhere

She's as pretty as passion.

She's as pretty as romance.

She's as pretty as a broken heart.

She's as pretty as a kiss.

I don't kiss my lovers, but I'd kiss her.

I'd love her.

She's as pretty as my love for her.

I cannot kiss you with the lights on

If holding hands is as far as you'll let me go,
I'll hold your hand forever

If we're only two friends sharing a hug, I'd be
your best friend for life

If you would like to kiss me, you can

But I cannot kiss you with the lights on

I crawl into your bed

Your skin melts into my arms

Your bedroom is dark with only my heart lit
up

It's like we're on the moon

My body inches closer to yours

It's like we're one

You fit your lips into mine

It's like we're a puzzle

a pretty thing in the middle of nowhere

I want to stay in this kiss forever

I want to die in this kiss

But when morning comes,

the sun reveals itself

exposing us

You lean in, and I step back

I fell out of the closet once before

And I've never stopped falling since

I fell out of the closet once before

And this reminds me of that

Because here I am,

Falling right into love with you

You lean in to kiss me

And I fall back

a pretty thing in the middle of nowhere

I cannot kiss you with the lights on

Because to kiss you with the lights on would mean to see your face

And to see your face would mean to know that you are a woman

Why admit that when we could simply turn the lights off?

We're sharing a bed tonight, for the first time

And you ask me, innocently,

"You want the lights on or off?"

sapphic

/ˈsafɪk/
adjective

>
> describing the romantic and
> sexual attraction I feel towards
> her.

Sapphic is a safe word.

I once called a bisexual girl a sapphic, and
she asked if I was calling her a slur.

"Yes, Granny, I'm writing another book. A
sapphic book." And my Catholic
grandmother smiles and brags to all of her
Catholic friends who can't wait to read my
book because they believe me when I say
that 'sapphic' simply means 'romance',

Sapphic is the magic word I use when I want to say,

"I'm bisexual, but men have treated me shitty in the past, so I've developed a preference for women. But I can't call myself a lesbian because I am not a lesbian. But I don't want to use the word 'bisexual' because I don't want to attract the men who will fetishise my sexuality and ask me for a threesome."

Sapphic is the magic word for when I want to say,

"I like girls!"

but the internalised homophobia begs me not to.

Mommy Issues

You are not a replacement for my mother. In fact, you are a constant, painful reminder of her. You're a man-eating bitch who writes poems as if they're spells from a witch. No, wait, that is my mother. No, wait, that's me. How'd I find myself where I swore I'd never be? When did I stop being able to tell the difference between my mother and me? I was never breastfed as a baby, so I'm making up for it as an adult. I searched for her in the women I loved. I cheated on boys and treated my friends like they were just background noise, all because I was scared to be hurt. I know that you'll leave me one day, because I couldn't even make my own mother stay. But I was fighting so much that I didn't even notice when I became my own enemy. Because when I turned 19 and my father told me, "You look just like your mother did at that age," I looked at my reflection and convinced myself, "No, this is just a phase!" I wasted all those years trying to escape her, but with every year I turned, my face replaced hers. How did I not see the signs? With one sentence, I describe her personality, and she describes mine. Why have we scribed the same line? Now, I'm a girl with a barrel of problems and the only person who can help me solve them is the woman who's been this girl before. I cut open my body to find my DNA, but instead I find my birth date. A day that brings together two twisted chains. A name for the baby girl who stole their faces. I can try to force myself into a new family; but at some point, at some age, some man will fall in love with my hand-me-down reflection and threaten to replicate.

13/12/23

hold my hand under the stars.

stop me from stumbling into the cars.

tonight i love the liquor, but trust my slurred words, girl, i love you more.

speak to me in a language our friends can't understand. leave 'em sitting on the soft grass.

i'll lean on this concrete wall, babe, you can lean on me.

you've been smoking all night. your words are shy, but your tongue is blunt as it hugs mine.

you taste like a cherry; how do i taste, baby?

steal my skin, possess my flesh.

kiss me as if it's our last breath.

Superhero

I am sorry for not coming to your
rescue earlier in life.
I am sorry for not knowing you when
you needed me.
I am sorry for not saving you from
monsters and villains.
I am sorry for not being your
superhero because I was too busy
being a stranger.

The Sunset Cloud Theory

I like to write down the little things

you say.

I turn your words into Bible verses.

Your tongue is one to be worshiped.

If your body is God, my heart is a

Christian; it waits for you to come.

You say, "When I die, I want to be a

sunset cloud."

And you get upset with me when I

say,

"I don't believe in an afterlife."

I don't believe in Heaven, but it must

be a place, because you had to have

fallen from somewhere.

I don't believe in God, but He must

exist,

because only He could make

something as precious as you.

I don't believe that clouds are the souls of people gone. But if they are, then when I die, I'll become a thunderstorm.

I don't believe that you will die one day.
But if you do, I'll look at a cloud when the sun sets, and I'll believe that it's you.

Spoil Me, Emotionally

Don't give me earrings.

Give me empathy.

Don't buy me flowers.

Shower me with stories about your day.

I don't need the material things to feel
loved.

Gift-giving isn't my language.

The only physical thing I need from you

is your touch.

Words of affirmation are the prayers of my
religion.

Don't spoil me with diamonds.

Just lay here and let me die in your arms.

I don't need a trip to Paris.

Take me home to your parents.

a pretty thing in the middle of nowhere

Don't buy me the expensive wine.

Put your red lips on mine.

Spoil me, rotten.

Bless me, unholy.

I don't like being spoilt,

it's rotten.

But if you insist on spoiling me,

spoil me emotionally.

Paper Flowers

Bouquets decay,

but these paper flowers of ours

will never wither away.

How to Swim: A Lover's Guide

I have always been afraid to swim.

I have been convinced that the water will pirouette around my feet and wet the sand so soggy that it will collapse beneath me; there will be no wave to push me back to safety.

It was such a relief to leave my mother's wet womb. But at age three, I was dunked into a pool so deep that I'm still coughing up the water eighteen years later.

It was such a relief to meet you on the pavement. To feel the grass beneath our feet as we share stories. To climb through broken doors and laugh in haunted halls.

I struggle to express my love sometimes; but the day a tsunami arrives, if only one breath is able to inhale before the water gags us, you can have mine.

a pretty thing in the middle of nowhere

Love *is*

knowing from the moment I met you,

and forgetting what it feels like to have

never known you. I'll choose you until

death hugs me. I'll think of you even

if age erases my memory. Nothing could

stop me from knowing that love is you.

(Never) mine

I am the sun – but she is the moon, the
stars, the birds, the rivers, and the sky.

She is the heart in my chest.

She is the oxygen keeping my lungs alive.

She is the best crush I've ever
accomplished.

She is the best lover I've ever failed.

She is the best thing a girl could have.

But I do not have her.

She belongs to herself, no matter how I try.

She is the best thing that will never be mine.

Because I am not the best thing she
deserves.

She deserves better, more than I can give
her.

Her face is an image sent to plague my mind.

Her voice is a broken record in my mind.

I want her, but she will never be mine.

"I love you," I say.

She looks up from her phone screen, "Sorry, what?"

"Never mind."

I still make her laugh, while I scream on the inside.

I still pretend to be okay with being just friends.

I'd rather be something small than nothing at all.

Part Two

To lose you, was to lose my sanity.

a pretty thing in the middle of nowhere

The worst heartbreaks

are those given to you by

the relationships you were never in.

There is no greater heartbreak

than when the person you love most

is the one who loves you the least.

To lose you, was to lose my sanity.

To love you, was to drive myself crazy.

"I love you…"

You used to say it first.

But now, you don't even say it back.

Breaking Up with Myself

"It's not you, it's me."

This is a phrase I've said too many times to people who hear it as a lie;

an easy escape from the relationship. But I swear I'm not jumping ship.

You see, it's me who will drown if I don't stop you from loving me.

So, I'm breaking up with me.

I'm breaking up with the me who believes in love at first sight.

The me who doesn't need to know your last name to fantasise that one day it will be mine.

I'm breaking up with the me who falls fast, falls hard.

a pretty thing in the middle of nowhere

The me who hits her head on the concrete
when she crashes.

The me who doesn't know the difference
between a relationship that is long-lasting

and a quick spark of passion.

I'm breaking up with the me who seeks
validation from men.

The me who believes that she must be
undressed to be loved.

The me who thinks that you won't want to
spend time with me unless you're inside of
me.

I'm breaking up with lust.

Affairs with men who don't love me enough
to stay if a baby tries to make its way.

Passion that I use as a weapon to steal love
that lasts sixty seconds.

The lust that I use as a drug to feed my addiction to self-destruction.

I'm breaking up with my ex.

Even though he broke up with me years ago,

I still held onto the hope that one day he'll change his mind.

Today, I am breaking up with that hope.

I'm breaking up with every bad habit I own.

Every dirty name I've ever called myself.

Every hateful rumour spread about me that I was insecure enough to believe.

I am breaking up with my insecurities.

"It's not you, it's me."

It's not you who is always there to wipe away my tears; it's me.

It's not you who comforts me at night when my fears are holding me too tight; it's me.

It's not you who will feel the consequences if I keep throwing my body over your electric fences; it's me.

So, I am breaking up with the version of myself you know too well.

Even if that means having to break up with you too.

a pretty thing in the middle of nowhere

Tears at Midnight

Dear Diary,

I have lost my lover.

To what? I remain unsure.

It could have been to the ring of my phone at 9:04p.m., delivering the letters of her fears and uncertainties. It could have been to her claims that she cannot be what I deserve, yet she has failed to realize that the only thing I long for is her. What I do not deserve is to have my heart sliced into two from its core. What I do not deserve is to be kept awake by taunting thoughts, as the voices convince me that this destruction of love is all my fault.

Salty drops bathe my face. These tears are my baptism. I have found a new faith. I no longer believe in love. Heartache has become my religion.

I no longer believe in my own attractiveness. Any hole can keep a man, but only a pretty soul can keep a woman. Perhaps I own something ugly. Our friendship is her priority; vengeance is mine.

"I value our friendship way too much to let you hate me in the long run."

I hate her right now. In the long run, she was supposed to be my bride.

I will now live in isolation and eat only myself from the inside. Hatred replaces her name in my brain, but beauty remains as the image of her face. I pen these words to my diary; I refuse to be the reason her phone rings. I hope that my silence is as torturing to her as her words were to me.

I want to blame myself. Maybe if I wasn't so needy, she'd want me more. Maybe if I wasn't so honest about my feelings. I feel naked. Maybe if I was clothed.

Tonight, I lost my lover to her inability to understand that it is a privilege to have *me* love her. I lost her to the consequences that she must now suffer. Tonight was the first time she made me cry. But I love her too much to let it be the last.

Sincerely, a bitch with a broken heart.

Distance, Silence

You're not speaking to me

I'm speaking to a shell that was once my
friend

my crush

has crushed me

I'm still waiting on that text from you

"Meet me in the bathroom"

I'm waiting on that apology

I'm waiting on your kiss

I'm waiting for things to go back

to how they used to be

I'm waiting for the past to become our future

How stupid of me

a pretty thing in the middle of nowhere

I fly to the moon just to bring it back for you

and you ask me, "Why?"

And not in the innocent

Do you like me or something?

way

But in the

*Why do you keep chasing me when I'm so
clearly pushing you away?*

way

You keep pushing me away

so I'll be going now.

Maybe you'll appreciate my love

when I start hating you.

Why make me feel unwanted

when you wanted me in the first place?

I Don't Want to Know You Anymore

You posted a picture

Disturbed my peaceful nature

I closed the app

I can't say that I didn't want to dial your
number after

Did you overthink before you posted?

I didn't comment; did you notice?

Don't answer; I don't want to know

I don't want to know you anymore

You bleached your hair – again

You went out with *our* friends

If I didn't know better, I'd think that you're
trying to pretend
We never kissed that night

a pretty thing in the middle of nowhere

But, hey, I'm alright

I'm raising my white flag in this war

I don't want to fight with you anymore

You told everyone that I was the one who left

Forgot to mention how you drained me till I bled

All over your bedroom floor

Telling your friends everything except how you broke me to my core

Where's the girl I fell for?

I don't know you anymore

Without you, I've never been saner

Falling out of love was like escaping danger

I looked for you and found a stranger

You called me, searching for closure

a pretty thing in the middle of nowhere

I blocked your number; I laid our love to rest

I burned your clothes; there's no reminders
of you left

I don't break promises; remember how I
promised to never hurt you first?

Now, I promise myself to know my worth

This isn't worth it anymore

I don't want to know you anymore!

The girl I met would've never broken my
heart

The girl I met, she used to grieve whenever
we were apart

The girl I met, she was sunshine, she was
fun

The girl I met would've hated who she's
become

a pretty thing in the middle of nowhere

I don't know that girl anymore.

Now your body is standing right in front of
me

Your face is missing; your lying lips, I refuse
to see

Call me prideful, call me spiteful, call me
crazed

Call me anything but my name

I don't know yours anymore.

Our Friends Are Laughing at Me

Did I accidentally tell another self-deprecating joke? Because I can hear our friends laughing at me!

Silly me. Stupid me! Obsessed with a girl who's obsessed with herself. And I can't even vent about it to my friends. Because they won't be on my side. They'll stay "neutral".

The next girls' trip to make it out of the group chat will be my funeral. I should just fucking die, since nobody cares to be on my side!

Jesus, I'm dramatic, aren't I?

Sorry for getting out of character; let me just tell a joke and everything will be alright. I wouldn't want to make anyone uncomfortable with my vulnerability. Okay, so, two studs walk into a bar …

I'm not a girl with feelings, am I? Nah, feelings are for weak bitches. I can't be crying over you; go from here with that lesbian shit. I'm just joking, girl, like always. You know I like how the pink tastes.

Do you hear that? I do.

I can hear our friends laughing at me when I plan a group date just to spend time with you and everyone shows up, except for you.

I can hear our friends laughing at me as they witness every interaction between us where I was being gay while you were just being a friend.

I can hear our friends laughing because they think that everything I say is a fucking joke. So, when I said, "I love you," you thought that was the punchline.

i let you break me

it's such a shame.

I really loved you.

No one's to blame.

Time to face the truth.

My intense emotions chased you

away.

You ran.

I was the one stupid enough to stay.

I wait for you to love me back,

But I forgot that love

feels like a heart attack.

You brought me pain.

I cried many nights.

I cried out blood.

and now I'm too weak to fight.

I want you to love me better.

But I can't make you change.

Perhaps I'm to blame

for the way I let you break me.

It's such a shame.

It's not your fault I couldn't make you love me

I don't ever leave when they mistreat
me, because what if I leave and they
don't miss me?
Our voices get lost in my memories.
Only pictures remain.
You know, I keep all our
conversations secured in my brain.
Wrote some of them down and
turned them into poems.
But your point of view stays missing.
I never understood your mind
anyway.
It's not my fault you gave me so
many treasures to keep.
It's not your fault I couldn't make you
love me.

Bad feminist

If I had a penis

You'd love me more

I call you my princess

You act like a whore

With men, never with me

I'm starting to think that you are guilty

Of being one of those girls who claim to
be bisexual

Yet you're too afraid to let me kiss you in
public

But he can pull out his dick,

And without hesitation, you suck it

Call me a bad feminist for saying it, but
I'll say it

You bitch!

a pretty thing in the middle of nowhere

Whenever I wear a skirt,

I don't feel like a girl

But I try to be pretty for you

I try and try,

While being a man is all that he has to

do

And I get mad when you talk about men

Who ask you on dates

While you tell your mother that *I'm* just a

friend

A friend who you invite to sleep over

And kiss under the sheets

If I were a man,

Would you go out on a date with me?

Call me a bad feminist for saying it, but

I'll say it

You bitch!

If I had a dick

I'd be allowed to marry you

I wouldn't have to write this

Write you poems about "what ifs"

What if I were a boy

Would I be a bad feminist for calling you

a bitch

Whenever I saw you with another man?

You're a bad feminist

Because if I were a boy, you'd hold my

hand

What if I had a penis, would you love me

more?

Would you suck it without hesitation?

You bitch!

What if this wasn't a poem about our

love

What if we were straight

Would I be a bad feminist for calling you

a bitch

Whenever you were a bad friend to me?

Would I be the bitch?

What if I didn't love you?

Would I be a bad feminist if I didn't fall in

love

With the most perfect woman to ever

exist?

Am I a bitch?

I'm a bad feminist

Because I'm using the word incorrectly

Feminism is about equality

Yet here I am,

Bitching about some bitch not loving me

Wishing that I were a man

Not for equal pay or respect

But for a girl who claims to *like* me

Because I bet, if I were a man, she
would claim to love me instead

Broken Soulmates

How could someone be so perfect
yet so wrong for you?
Why do we fall in love with people
who aren't our soulmates?
I don't understand love
Because people love differently
So you have to learn how to love
them properly
And teach them how to love you
But aren't soulmates supposed to be
made for each other?
If I have to learn you, it means that
we're not made for each other.
Are we not soulmates?
Am I so broken that another soul
can't complete me?
Is it your fault that you can't fix me?
Or is it my fault for being broken?

Accept it and move on

I have accepted that I still love you
I will not fight it
But I will not act on it either
I will simply accept what I have been
denying for months and move on

I have also accepted that you don't
love me
I will not force or manipulate you to
I will simply accept what I have been
pretending was not true for years

It is possible that, one day, you will
begin to love me
It may or may not happen

It is certain that, one day, I will stop
loving you
It will happen

My Sweet Girl

I wasted so much time,
but time healed my cuts.
I gave you everything,
yet you never gave a fuck.

Guess it's my fault for loving your
lust.
Attachment to ashes, trust to dust.

Goodbye forever, my sweet girl.
Where will you ruin next,
now that you've destroyed my world?

You Bring Out the Worst in Me

Honestly speaking,
you bring out the worst in me.
I have carefully created a
comfortable persona for myself,
but somehow,
you see right through it.

You bring out the parts of me that
I've worked tirelessly to bury.
The parts of me that crave a physical
touch that is something more than a
quick fuck.
The parts of me that only partially
like men.
The parts of me that don't need to
use humour every time I want to cry.
Those are all the parts of me that I
do not like.

I tried to change myself into

someone (I thought) you'd prefer,

but that only pushed you away.

I don't want to be myself around you,

because I've tried so many times to

kill her –

and failed.

I tried to change myself into

somebody I'd prefer,

and now I don't know who I am;

I only know my name.

My friends always call me

delusional,

But I am only that by choice.

My heart is delusional

because my mind constantly lives in

the reality of our situation,

and it drives me fucking insane.

You always say that I'm assertive.

But I am only that by force.

I only chase after what I want

because I've never been the girl who

attracts.

For a quick second in every day,

you make me feel wanted.

But then I get too *assertive*,

and you pull away.

You like my confidence;

I wonder if you'd still like me if you

knew that it was fake.

I wonder if you'd still laugh if you
knew that my jokes are only funny
because I'm disturbed and in pain.

You make me want to love you,
and I hate that.
My tongue is obsessed with your
name, so I curse it every night.

Now we argue all the time
over nothingness,
and I'm always the one to start it.
I just need one reason to call you
after midnight.
So, I'll spot the tiniest issue
and start an entire war.
I'll show my closet of ugly and beg
you to compliment my beauty.

Honestly,

you bring out the worst in me.

Because you represent everything

I've always feared:

falling for somebody who sees the

good, the bad, and the crazy,

and still likes me.

Somebody who makes me

want to be

the Sun;

not the fire.

I have two choices – either lose you,

or accept my identity.

As I watch you leave because you'd

rather be alone than with one of my

multiple personalities,

I fear that you've already made the

decision for me.

Friendship Island

I live on Friendship Island, all alone.

I live in a box, and I don't have a cell phone, so when something happens in my friends' lives, I'm always the last to know.

I live on their roofs, so I'm always there whenever they need me. But they never open the doors and windows.

I live in a coffin that remains unvisited. I'm a body hungry for company; yet I remain unfed. My remains will probably be smoked by my friends.

To everyone else, a friend is just a friend. To me, a friend is a home. So, I live on Friendship Island. I have many friends, yet somehow, I live here alone.

Pretty Girl

They tell you, "You don't have to be
smart, kind, or ambitious. You just
have to be pretty, girl."

And the second you start to believe
that, they say,
"You're so stupid, self-centred and
lazy. All you care about is being
pretty, girl."

They watch men abuse you
But it'll be all your fault because,
"You shouldn't have looked so
pretty, girl."

Eventually, your soft skin will fade
into bitter dust.
"It's such a shame what she
became. She used to be such a
pretty girl."

Go To Hell

See,

what you don't realise is,

I only tell you to go to Hell

because

I want us to be together for eternity.

Never Made Love

I've had sex many times, but I've never made love.

I was the product of a teenage love affair, and they swear that I was made from love.

But my parents broke up when I was born, so I guess when my mother made me,

she didn't make love.

So many men I've given myself to; so many times when my body wasn't enough.

I could always see their potential, but I could never see my own worth.

a pretty thing in the middle of nowhere

I always mend my own broken heart; I always convince myself that it doesn't hurt.

And it's nice to smile until my face hurts; until it hurts.

It's nice to turn a blind eye to your actions, as I hang on to your every false word.

Would you like a tiny bottle-necklace with my blood in it?

Or would you like me to keep distance between us and pretend to not give a shit?

Sorry I didn't reply to you; I thought you dropped dead like I told you to.

Sorry I keep apologising for things that aren't my fault. Sorry I keep confusing words of affirmations with verbal assault.

a pretty thing in the middle of nowhere

Sorry I fell in love with you,

You must be exhausted.

Sorry I have all these problems.

Sorry you caused it.

The mind of a lonely girl

Relationships aren't for me. I'm no good at them.

I'm good at craving them.

imagining them.

leaving them.

But I'm not good at being in them.

It's the little things I'm not good at.

I'm not good at hugging you when you need to be hugged.

I'm not good at keeping you company when I need time for myself.

I'm not good at holding hands.

I'm not good at apologising when *you're* in the wrong.

a pretty thing in the middle of nowhere

It's the big things I'm not good at.

I'm not good at being faithful.

I'm not good at feeling like I'm enough for you.

I'm not good at trusting your voice when it resembles past lies.

I'm good at saying, "I love you" even when I know that you'll never say it back.

I'm good at planning our wedding before we have a first date.

I'm good at avoiding fights because I'm good at avoiding.

Relationships aren't good for me because I've never been in a good relationship.

I've never been loved with certainty.

I've never been chosen first.

But I think I've cracked the code –

If you have a fear of abandonment, just
keep doing things that pushes people away.
That way, when they leave, at least you'll
know why.

I think some people were born to be alone.

Relationships aren't for everyone.

I mean, who would write poems if people
never got their hearts broken?

Ring

According to our friends, there's a shiny new ring around your finger. You wear it everywhere. Yet I've never seen it. Do I not deserve to? Perhaps you think that I'd be jealous; try to break it? Pardon my questions, I know you prefer that type of silence that drives me mad. But I just need to ask, what's so un-special about me that I cannot see this fine jewel? Why must you treat me like I'm just a person you know, instead of one you love? You want to shut me out? Shut up and go away! Because you're not sorry and I'm not sane! You can keep your secret ring and your stone-cold ways. You're not a real friend, and I'm not really in the mood to play games. I tried to give us a happy ending, and I can lie to myself, but I refuse to lie to my pen. I'm not happy. We're not friends. The end.

Part Three

To let you go, was to forgive myself if you

never came back.

I'll Never Know Beauty Again

I fell in love with a pretty girl, and she made me think of you. It's hard to miss a stranger, but I'll never stop missing you. I know the years have forgotten us for a reason, and you're not the type to hold onto these tiny, faded moments, but I'll hold onto them for us. I'll hold onto us and wish that I could've held onto you.
I fell in love with a girl as pretty as the moon, and it reminded me of the time I fell for you. Not love, but a like so strong that it exposed my secrets. Back when we were sixteen, skipping biology, questioning our chemistry. The day before my seventeenth birthday, you took a picture of us, but I've never seen it. I hope you've kept our picture safe. I haven't seen you since that day.

But every time that I declare my love for her, I remember being fifteen, whispering that I liked you.
I saw a pretty girl today and I almost held my breath, mistaking her for you. With *her*, I know love, patience, frustration, and forgiveness. But because of *you*, I know beauty. And because I haven't seen you in years, I fear that I'll never know beauty again.

Then I Saw Her Again

And then,

I saw you again.

But we weren't sixteen anymore.

I saw you for the first time, all over again.

But this time, we weren't standing together at the back of the class on the first day of secondary school in September. This time, you were waving at me from the other side of the office.

I met you for the first time, again. Because this time, you weren't a boy-crazy teenager; you were a few years away from having a teenager of your own. I missed you for four years. But for one week, you were mine again.

But then, I quit the job, and we stood
in the bathroom of a bar,

and for the second time, that was
the last time I saw you.

You're busy posting beautiful
pictures of your beautiful family.
Meanwhile, I'm busy writing an
ocean of poems for another
beautiful woman.

But I would not have had the
courage to love her, if I never had
the nerve to like you.

...

I saw Beauty again, but I didn't know
her anymore.

The sun set over the bar, and Beauty
stood in front of me; but the moon
was all I could see.

WYD tonight?

I stopped the movie because I didn't want to watch it without you. I've stopped smiling whenever you're not around because I have no reason to. Never again would I let a girl into my heart. From your lips you said goodnight and I tried to fall asleep but without you lying next to me, I know no peace. Baby girl, please text me tonight before I close my eyes. Forever, I'll miss you. Forever, I'll wait for you. But before forever comes, what are you doing tonight?

Always The Poet

I'm always writing the eulogies of my friends. There will be no words left when *I'm* dead. There will be no more friends. I was put on this earth to write. Not my own story, but the stories of the voiceless humans. I was born to be a pen. Always the writer, never the story. When I was younger, I thought that my parents were just strangers to each other, only meeting on my birth certificate. I was born to be the child in a family that did not exist. Always the lover, never the loved. When I was a little girl, I wanted to be famous. I wanted to be loved. Even if it was by strangers. So, I wrote songs and poems and novels and letters to be read by my grandchildren. They'll engrave my poetry on my obituary, and maybe then, maybe when I'm dead, someone will write a poem about me.

unmute the muse

Dear reader, I dare you to question the poet. She speaks her truth, but before you call me a liar, I dare you to read *my* lyre poetry. I loved the sun so much that I became its flower. How dare she question my loyalty? I may be sleeping next to someone new, but ask her how many men she slept under while swearing that I was her moon. Maybe I triggered something from her past, but ask me about the history *I* had to forget. Maybe my scars healed quicker, but that doesn't mean I never bled.

Dear reader, I hope that you enjoy the poet's point of view. I may be her muse, but did you ever stop to ask if I wrote poems too?

a pretty thing in the middle of nowhere

Don't Tell Your Girlfriend

I think I like you, but don't tell your girlfriend.

She won't like me anymore.

Our friendship would fall apart,

and everyone will blame me for her broken
heart,

and I wouldn't care because I don't want
friends;

all I want is you.

But don't tell your girlfriend I said that.

Don't tell your girlfriend that I smile
whenever you text me.

That, whenever I see your name across my
phone screen,

my heart forgets how to function and skips a
beat.

a pretty thing in the middle of nowhere

Don't tell your girlfriend that I ask you about your day,

and that I wish it was spent with me.

Don't tell her how we used to flirt

before you got into a relationship and ruined my fantasies.

Don't tell her that I still fantasise about you.

Don't tell her what you think of me.

Tell me, what do you think of me?

Do you think I'm a horrible person for wanting you?

Do you think if she was out of the picture, you'd want me too?

What would you do if I were to kiss you?

Don't tell your girlfriend that I ask you these questions.

a pretty thing in the middle of nowhere

Don't tell your girlfriend that I'm putting
myself in this position

to be her shadow, never her replacement.

I know you love her; I'll settle for a quick kiss
on the pavement.

Don't tell your girlfriend that I don't know my
worth.

I know that she's your girlfriend and you're
hers,

but tell her that *I* wanted you first.

river of tears

I judge my love for you based on how much
I've cried for you.

How many times, how many tears.

How many buckets I could fill if I went one
day without hearing your voice.

If I thought you were upset with me, would I
cry a drizzle or would I cry a thunderstorm?

There is no other person I've cried over as
much as I've cried for you.

All I have left to give you is this river of tears
I've shed for you.

But every single night that I cry myself to
sleep,

I wonder –

even if it was only once, only a drizzle -

have you ever cried over me?

suicide before another heartbreak

Dear new love,

I've been labelled, 'Damaged Goods'.

I've been haunted by ex-lovers, and taunted by my friends –

"I can't believe you used to love them!"

I can't believe it either.

I can't believe that I'm in love again,

But I will welcome you with open arms and allow my heart to love again.

But listen,

This is the last time that I will be in love for the first time.

She was my last heartbreak, my last "goodbye", my last "we can still be friends".

I have enough old lovers and enough
new friends.

I have had enough of the betrayals, and
the mind games, and the first dates that
end.

Dear new love,

To make me feel 'in love' again, is to
make me feel suicidal.

I'd put the gun to my head because I'd
rather be dead than claim another ex.

I don't want you to hurt me, so I'll hurt
me instead.

I'll put the knife to my wrists; nothing
hurts more than missing your kiss.

I don't want to end my life,

But I don't have the strength to go
through another heartbreak.

a pretty thing in the middle of nowhere

So, if you are going to love me, love me right.

Because, if I go to sleep with a broken heart tonight,

I won't wake up alive.

a pretty thing in the middle of nowhere

I once saw a girl with curly, pink hair.

She sat in front of me in class, and for months I never saw her face.

I didn't know her name, but I knew her pink hair and the black ink on her back.

I tried to search for her face, but I found it nowhere.

I once met a girl with black butterfly locs.

Eyes like a crescent moon, lips like strawberry gloss.

Every time I'd try to speak to her, my only words were a Cheshire cat smile.

I found her old photos with her curly, pink hair.

I once met a girl that I saw before, but I couldn't remember where.

I once wrote a poem for a girl with a
boyfriend.

I was floating in love with her,

often having to catch myself from falling,

I made my own version of her to exist in
my poem.

I once wrote a poem for a girl,

and then I wrote her book.

I once took a picture of a girl on the
beach.

She stood with her long, honey-blonde
braids in front of the sea.

She always changes her hair, but she
never changes her boyfriend.

I took a picture of her with my eyes; an
image that haunts my mind every night.

She had scars on her body as if she had been through a war. Yet she never fought for me.

Dimples in her cheeks whenever she smiled. So I noticed every moment I wasn't making her happy.

She was like a mermaid, ruled by the ocean of her emotions.

But I was a lion, unable to swim.

For me, falling in love was like starting a fire.

I once met a mermaid, I feared would leave me drowning in her sea of nowhere.

I once became friends with a girl who laughed at everything I said.

The more she laughed, the more I spoke.

I didn't have a pretty face like hers, but I had my jokes.

And if my humour was the thing that made her like me,

I'd never be serious, never be vulnerable, never be weak.

Her hair was still honey-blonde, but now her boyfriend was gone.

Out of nowhere, she started flirting with me.

I didn't want anything to go wrong, so I used my humour as a shield.

I tried to protect our friendship.

Whenever we would cross the street, I'd hold her hand. I tried to protect her.

But the first time my eye twitched when she spoke about a new boy she liked,

I realised that I had forgotten to protect myself.

And now I was sitting by a water fountain with my walls up, waiting for my mermaid to come break them down.

She came from nowhere.

I once kissed a girl who saw kissing as a casual thing.

She knew that I didn't kiss people because it's too intimate. She knew that intimacy was my greatest fear.

Intimacy births attachment, and attachment always leaves me abandoned.

But she kissed me anyway, and to her, it was just a kiss.

But to me, it was the night I lost everything I was trying to keep protected.

I once saw a flower on the ground.

It was blown to me by the wind.

It was pretty, like the apple Eve bit.

I gave the flower to the girl who was the cherry of my sins.

It was fragile, like our friendship.

It was pink, like her hair was once.

And like my feelings for her, it came to me from nowhere.

I once loved a girl who changed her hair colour like she changed her mind.

She said she'd leave me, but I think she changed her mind.

If I could ask my future self anything, I'd ask her about that girl. Do I still know her? Am I still writing her poems?

I once loved a girl who led me on.

She led me on, but she led me away from my toxic ex.

She led me on, but she led me into a habit of changing my self-destructive ways because I wanted to be a better person for her.

She led me on, but she led me into nights where I cried over her so much that I had no choice but to accept my love for girls.

I once loved a girl.

a pretty thing in the middle of nowhere

I once found a pretty thing in the middle of nowhere.

I watered it, even when it was drowning me.

I protected it, even when I was weak.

It gave me promises in exchange for my fears.

It said, "I love you"; and in exchange, I believed. I cared.

But in the end,

it died

and left me holding its corpse,

lost

in the middle of nowhere.

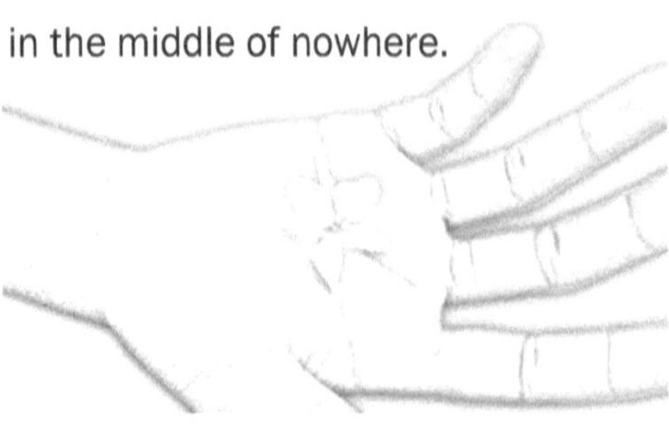

Lockets

I own rare lockets, but it is not their diamond shells that make them special. Inside each, there are candid paintings - those are my treasures.

Some of the faces, I met when we were teens. Some I met when I still smiled with my first set of teeth. All I plan to know until life no longer knows me.

I own quite a few lockets; but numbers matter not. They drape down to my chest, the best place for matters of the heart. These lockets tell many stories. Some longer than the rest. Live in the moment but capture a snippet. What is merely a picture now, will one day be museums for our children. Each locket I own, I wear them with pride. Wedding rings come and go, but these lockets will always be mine.

The One That Got Away

I can't help but think about how beautiful we would've been together if only I was enough for you.

Everybody keeps giving me advice on what to do with you. They cheer me on as I continue to portray myself as the love-sick fool.

"Chase her, show her that you want her,"

they say,

"You don't want her to be the one that got away."

I'm always the one begging love to stay.

I'm always the one they can never get rid of. The one they kiss, use, leave, recycle, but never love.

I've been trying my hardest since the day

I met you.

I try and try, and you try to push me

away,

and I'm too stubborn to let you.

I'm tired now. I waited for you,

I watched you try to push me again,

and for once, I let myself fall back.

My mind snapped back to reality

when my head hit the bricks.

It's time to let go of this fantasy I keep

clinging to.

But when our friends ask "Who was the

one that got away?"

Make sure you tell them that it was me,

not you.

I only walked out the door because you

left it open. I tried to lock it.

I gave you a locket and keys to my heart.

Yours was a precious cold metal,

only in your chest for decoration.

Your love was a plastic piece of art.

I'm always getting abandoned,

so now I'm forced to switch the
dynamics.

I've always been afraid to set my lovers
free.

What if I regret it?

What if I wasted time on someone who
never belonged to me?

But my heart has too many bandages on
it now,

I can't risk another wound.

You control us; letting you go is the only
thing *I* have the power to do.

To let you go, is to promise to forgive myself if you never come back.

So, I promise. I promise my heart there'll be no more cracks.

I may be falling apart as I pen this, but everything will fall into place one day.

Congratulations

on being the first lover to break me so deeply

that I finally found the strength to get away.

Love, T

And then one day, you met someone else, and you were happy, and you looked through the window and saw the Moon.

And I was in love with my reflection, and I was at peace, and I looked through the window and saw the Sun.

And we both realized that we were never meant to exist in the same sky.

When the eclipse came to an end, and I saw you again, I didn't see the perfect girl I was hopelessly in love with. I didn't see the evil bitch who broke my heart.

I looked at you and I saw my friend.

And she was enough for me,

and I was enough for her.

- Love, T

ABOUT THE AUTHOR

TAMARA ALI is a Trinidadian writer and professional daydreamer. Though she has been writing since the first day her fingers wrapped around a pencil in primary school, Tamara made her debut into the world of published authors at just nineteen years old, with her YA contemporary novel, *Red Like Love*. Now in her twenteens, Tamara has decided to take her purple pen pals on a journey beyond fiction, with her first collection of poetry. Her writing sessions usually include pop music playing in the background and a stack of snacks on standby. Tamara can be found on Instagram and TikTok @girlwiththepurplepen, or tamarabrianaali.wixsite.com/tamaraali.

www.ingramcontent.com/pod-product-compliance
Lightning Source LLC
Chambersburg PA
CBHW020734160726
47993CB00006B/2446